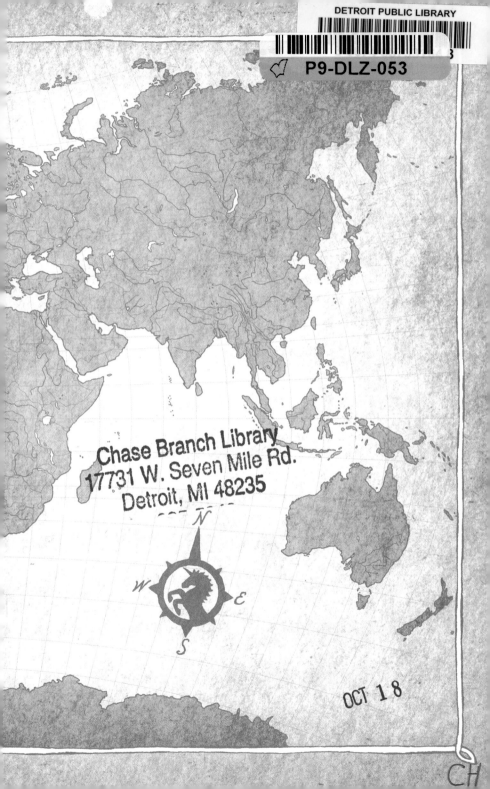

THE UNICORN RESCUE SOCIETY

THE CREATURE OF THE PINES

ALSO BY
ADAM GIDWITZ

A Tale Dark and Grimm

In a Glass Grimmly

The Grimm Conclusion

The Inquisitor's Tale:
Or, The Three Magical Children
and Their Holy Dog

THE UNICORN RESCUE SOCIETY
THE CREATURE OF THE PINES

BY **Adam Gidwitz**

ILLUSTRATED BY **Hatem Aly**

CREATED BY **Jesse Casey, Adam Gidwitz, and Chris Smith**

DUTTON CHILDREN'S BOOKS

DUTTON CHILDREN'S BOOKS

Penguin Young Readers Group
An imprint of Penguin Random House LLC
375 Hudson Street
New York, NY 10014

CIP Data is available.

Printed in the United States of America
ISBN 9780735231702

1 3 5 7 9 10 8 6 4 2

Edited by Julie Strauss-Gabel
Design by Anna Booth
Text set in Legacy Serif ITC Std

UNICORNS ARE REAL.

At least, I think they are.

Dragons are definitely real. I have seen them. Chupacabras exist, too. Also Sasquatch. And mermaids—though they are *not* what you think.

But back to unicorns. When I, Professor Mito Fauna, was a young man, I lived in the foothills of Peru. One day, there were rumors in my town of a unicorn in danger, far up in the mountains. At that instant I founded the Unicorn Rescue Society—I was the only member—and set off to save the unicorn. When I finally located it, though, I saw that it was *not* a unicorn, but rather a qarqacha, the legendary two-headed llama of the Andes. I was very slightly disappointed. I rescued it anyway. Of course.

Now, many years later, there are members of the Unicorn Rescue Society all around the world. We are sworn to protect all the creatures of myth and legend. Including unicorns! If we ever find them! Which I'm sure we will!

But our enemies are powerful and ruthless, and we are in desperate need of help. Help from someone brave and kind and curious, and brave. (Yes, I said "brave" twice. It's important.)

Will you help us? Will you risk your very *life* to protect the world's mythical creatures?

Will you join the Unicorn Rescue Society?

I hope so. The creatures need you.

Defende Fabulosa! Protege Mythica!

Mito Fauna, DVM, PhD, EdD, etc.

CHAPTER ONE

Elliot Eisner stood at the front of the bus, looking down the long aisle. Every seat was full. The other children scowled at him.

At least, Elliot was pretty sure they were scowling at him. He was the new kid, starting school three weeks into the new school year. *Who starts a new school three weeks into the year?* he thought. *Three weeks! It's far too late to make friends. The year is practically over!* Elliot considered turning around and walking back to his new house, where his mom and grandma were unpacking boxes. But that would just make things worse. Tomorrow, when he was forced to come back to school, he would be the kid who'd flipped out and run away on his first day. Not a good first impression.

Worst of all, his class was going on a field trip. On his very first day at school. Things just weren't supposed to work like that. He wasn't *prepared.*

Elliot sighed and began to walk slowly down the length of the bus. Maybe there were a couple of empty seats in the back. The kids stared at him. He slouched past. *They think I'm a weirdo.*

This made no sense. Elliot was not a weirdo. He was a normal kid. A little pale, kinda skinny, lots of curly brown hair. Pretty normal. But Elliot did not feel normal. Not on his first day at a new school, on a field trip he was not prepared for, surrounded by kids he did not know.

There *were* some empty seats in the back.

One was next to a big boy with a shaved head,

who smiled at him and then farted. Elliot would not be sitting there.

There was a seat next to a girl who was digging in her nose like she'd lost something. Then, she found it. Elliot would not be sitting there, either.

Finally, he saw a seat in the very last row, next to a girl who looked like the lead singer in a punk rock band. She wore a gray jean jacket and gray jeans and red high-tops, and her hair was an explosion of black twists. The girl was rocking back and forth like she was listening to music. But there were no earphones in her ears.

Punk rock Beethoven, Elliot thought. *This one thinks she's a punk rock Beethoven. But at least she's not finding buried treasure up her nose or playing the tuba through her butt.*

He sat down next to her. She stopped rocking. "Hi," she said. "I'm Uchenna."

"I'm Elliot. I'm new here." *Obvious!* Elliot silently shouted at himself. *Don't say things that are obvious!* "This is my first day." *Everybody knows that!* "Even though school started three weeks ago." *Why are you stating facts that everyone knows?!?!*

Uchenna said, "I was new last year. I didn't start school till after Christmas."

You see, she knew—Wait, what?

Then Elliot said, "I thought I was the only person so horrendously unlucky to be forced to start a new school in the middle of the year."

Uchenna threw her head back and laughed. "No," she said. "There's two of us."

And that is how Elliot Eisner and Uchenna Devereaux became friends.

CHAPTER TWO

The class's teacher was Miss Vole.

Elliot liked to memorize books about animals—it was one of his hobbies—so he knew that voles are kind of like mice, but even smaller, with tiny eyes and plump little bodies. As Miss Vole stood up from her seat at the front of the bus, Elliot leaned over to Uchenna and whispered, *"Isn't it weird that she looks just like her name?"*

Uchenna smiled. "I think about that all the time."

Miss Vole cleared her voice. "Now, children," she said. She spoke like they were in kindergarten. She made her eyes very large, and if her voice got any higher, only dogs would be able to hear her. "Children, I expect you to be on your *very best* behavior." *Very best* was just about in dogs-only territory. "We have a *special* guest with us today for our *field trip*."

MISS VOLE

VOLE

Uchenna put her fingers in her ears so her eardrums wouldn't explode. Elliot snickered and did the same.

Miss Vole went on, "His name is Professor Fauna." It sounded like *Fow*-na. "Can you say *Professor Fauna*?"

"Why wouldn't we be able to say that?" Elliot whispered. Uchenna laughed and then shoved her fist into her mouth to stifle the sound.

"Professor Fauna," the children chanted.

And then, the professor stepped onto the bus, and it was as if a shadow had fallen over the whole class. Uchenna stopped laughing at once. Elliot gripped the green vinyl of the seat.

The professor was tall, with a thick beard that was half black, half gray. His hair stood up from his scalp like he was in the habit of kissing electric eels. He wore a threadbare tweed suit and leather shoes that looked like they had been really fancy once, long ago.

"*Buenos días, mis amigos,*" he said. His voice sounded like someone had put rocks in a blender.

Uchenna leaned over to Elliot. She wasn't smiling anymore. "He's a social studies teacher here. Everyone's terrified of him. They say he's totally unhinged from reality."

"Is he dangerous?" Elliot asked. He didn't like things that were dangerous unless they were animals, and he only liked dangerous animals if he was memorizing facts about them from a book.

Uchenna shrugged. "Maybe."

"Good morning," said Professor Fauna, and he rolled his *R*s so much, *morning* had four syllables. "I am Mito Fauna. You may call me Professor Fauna, Doctor Fauna, or Doctor Doctor

Fauna, since I am both a Doctor of Veterinary Medicine, with a specialty in large and rare species, and a Doctor of Philosophy, with a specialty in global mythology. In Germany, they call me Herr Doktor Doktor Professor, but you do not need to do that, because it takes too long, and it sounds silly. Also, I am not German, but Peruvian. Do you understand?"

Every child said "No," at exactly the same time.

"Excellent," the professor replied, evidently not hearing them. "Miss Vole has asked me to be your guide today on this field trip to the Pine Barrens of New Jersey. You will listen to me."

All the children nodded.

"You will do what I say."

They still nodded.

"If not, you will *DIE!*"

The children sat straight up in their seats.

"Not that I will kill you," Professor Fauna

added. "But there are many dangerous things in the Pine Barrens of New Jersey! So be careful, and do *exactly* as I tell you."

No one on the bus said a word. But silently, every child decided that, yes, they better do whatever this terrifying teacher said.

CHAPTER THREE

The bus drove from their school down the highway. They passed a big building with a maze of pipes and tanks and vats attached to it. Hundreds of chimneys spewed smoke high into the air. Across one of the big white vats ran the words: SCHMOKE INDUSTRIES, MAKING THE WORLD THE WAY WE WANT IT TO BE.

Elliot reached below his seat and dug through his backpack. He pulled out a bar wrapped in shiny foil.

"What's that?" Uchenna asked.

"It's a snack bar." Elliot held it out to her. It looked like nuts glued together with honey. "My mom and grandma make them for me. This is from my mom, because it doesn't have raisins. My grandma always puts raisins in the bars she makes."

"Interesting."

Elliot eyed Uchenna skeptically. "Do you really think that's interesting? Or are you being sarcastic?"

"No, I think it's interesting. Grandmas are wrinkly, usually. Raisins are wrinkly, always. Coincidence? Of course not."

"No, I definitely think it's a coincidence."

Uchenna pondered for a moment. "Nah. No way. Conspiracy." She started drumming on the back of the big green seat in front of them. Her hands picked up speed, thumping with her left and tapping with her right. And then, to Elliot's great surprise, she started to sing. Quietly and melodically:

"Old ladies are like raisins,
   Not just because they're sweet tastin'.
   Some are brown,
   Some are golden,
   All of them are wrinkly,
   And most of all . . . they're amazin'!"

Uchenna stopped singing.

"Old ladies are 'sweet tasting'?" said Elliot.

"Yeah, that part needs some work," Uchenna muttered.

The big yellow bus pulled into a dirt parking lot. There were no other cars or buses there. The children filed off and stood in a clump.

Pine trees, tall and crooked and scraggly, stood in a line around the edge of the parking area. The wind blew dust into their faces.

"Children!" Miss Vole said, and somewhere a dog woke up. "It's time to follow Professor Fauna!"

The professor led the group to the beginning of a trail. An old map, tattered, yellowed, and torn straight through the middle, was pinned to a crumbling plywood bulletin board. Elliot stopped and squinted up at the map.

"What are you doing?" Uchenna asked.

"I like to memorize maps when I go somewhere new, so I'll know how to make an escape,"
Elliot replied.

"Why would you need to make an escape?"
said Uchenna.

"You never know."

"How true," said a deep voice behind them.
They spun around. The professor was peering
down from under his weed-like eyebrows. "You
may indeed need to make an escape from the Pine
Barrens, for as I have said, they can be deadly.
But don't bother trying to memorize that map.

Between the many forkings of the roads, and the fire cuts that *look* like roads but are *not*, it is almost impossible to find your way out. It is almost like . . . *a trap*." Professor Fauna smiled at them broadly, and then suddenly turned away.

Elliot and Uchenna watched the professor start for the woods. "Why would he say that?" Elliot asked. "Teachers are supposed to be reassuring. That was the opposite of reassuring."

Uchenna just stared after the professor, shaking her head. "They say his office is a torture chamber, under the school. No one's allowed in it. Even the janitors."

"Whoa."

"Also," she added, "I heard he believes in unicorns."

CHAPTER FOUR

The path they followed was dry and sandy, like most of the soil in the Pine Barrens. That's why it's called "barren"—because most things can't grow in soil like that. But pine trees can, and they crowded in on the path, squeezing out the sunlight. Up and down the trunks, branches stuck out at crazy angles, with bristling needles at the ends. Long beards of gray-green moss hung down, making the trees look like old men. The cicadas hummed so loudly they sounded angry.

Elliot and Uchenna were in front, just behind the teachers. Suddenly, Professor Fauna spun around. He towered over the children. Elliot and Uchenna froze.

"The Pine Barrens is not a safe place," the professor intoned, his voice echoing over the gloomy path. "Many dangers are here. There are bears and coyotes and bobcats."

"*What?*" Elliot exclaimed under his breath.

"Cool!" said Uchenna.

"What?" he said again, but this time to Uchenna.

"I want to see a bobcat!"

"No, you don't," Elliot said. "Do you know that if a bear attacks you, you're supposed to play dead? But if you're attacked by a bobcat, you have to *fight it*. I don't want to fight a bobcat!"

Uchenna shrugged, as if she hadn't made up her mind on the question.

"Also," Professor Fauna went on, "the timber rattlesnake lives here. It is very deadly. So please, stay on the path."

With one movement, everyone in the class stepped away from the underbrush. No teacher had ever gotten his students to walk single file so easily.

Despite the dry earth, the ground was thick with green growth. They passed red-leafed huckleberries and sheep laurel, sweet fern and catbrier. There was a low footbridge over a stream. The water was brown.

"The water looks like tea!" someone said.

"Yeah, the water looks like pee!" said the farting boy from the bus. A few children chortled.

Fauna spun on the farting boy. "Your pee looks like this? Brown?"

The boy stammered.

"You should see a doctor, I think."

Now *all* the children laughed.

"This water is very special," the professor went on. "They call it cedar water, and it is brown because it is rich with cedar sap and iron. It is very sweet. Sea captains used to put it in barrels and take it to sea, because it would stay pure and sweet longer than any other water."

Uchenna peered over the bridge railing.

"Also," Fauna went on, "there are treasure ships sunk in the deeper rivers. Pirates would drag the ships into the Barrens, and no one would dare follow them."

"Is there still pirate gold?" someone asked.

"Perhaps! But there are greater treasures than gold in these woods." And then he stared into the pines, as if he'd lost something that he hoped, very soon, to find.

CHAPTER FIVE

As Professor Fauna led the class farther into the Barrens, the trees became shorter and shorter, and the ground became wet. Dragonflies buzzed among the plants. Everything smelled wet and rotten.

"There are also swamps in the Pine Barrens," Professor Fauna explained as they walked. "The swamp ground is too wet for most plants. But look at this."

He bent down. The children crowded around

him. Miss Vole said, "Not too close, children! Not too close!" They ignored her.

Professor Fauna's thick fingers were touching the weirdest plant Elliot and Uchenna had ever seen. It looked like a small green pot, with purple spots all over it. "This, children, is a pitcher plant. It is carnivorous. Which means, it eats meat."

Everyone's eyes went wide.

"You see," Professor Fauna went on, "the pitcher plant is very beautiful, and very often insects want to land on the pot-like part, to see if it has nectar inside for them to drink. But the sides of this little pot are very slippery, and the insects fall in. And what do you think is inside this little pot?"

Uchenna's hand shot in the air, and without waiting to be called on, she cried, "Poison!"

"Uchenna!" Miss Vole exclaimed. "Be serious! Of course there isn't *poison* in there!" Then she looked up at Professor Fauna. "Wait, *is* there poison in there?"

The professor gazed at Uchenna. "Ah, Miss Vole," he said, his eyes never leaving Uchenna, "there is indeed poison in this plant. The insects fall into the pot and are poisoned. Then they decompose, and the plant sucks the nutrients from their bodies." His voice became very quiet. His dark eyes remained fixed on Uchenna. He whispered, *"It is a trap."*

Then he straightened up, brushed off his worn tweed jacket, and said, "Did you know that many Christmas decorations come from the Pine Barrens? Come, let me show you!"

Elliot and Uchenna stared after him. *"Who* is *this guy?"* whispered Elliot.

"I told you," Uchenna replied. *"He's a social studies teacher."*

CHAPTER SIX

Professor Fauna led the class through the dark marsh, where the sky became just a small gray sliver between the pines. "In the old days," he was saying, "they found iron in the rivers and smelted it at furnaces. But today, they mostly grow cranberries and blueberries. And those Christmas decorations I mentioned! Pinecones, laurel, holly . . ."

Elliot and Uchenna had fallen to the back as they gazed at the gloomy swamp.

A dragonfly buzzed between them.

Somewhere, a branch cracked and fell to the wet earth.

Then, deep in the trees, something growled.

Elliot stopped walking. *"Good gracious!"* he whispered.

Uchenna cocked her head. "Did you just say 'Good gracious'?"

Elliot blushed. "Yeah. . . . My grandma won't let me use words worse than that."

Suddenly, the growling erupted into an angry snarl.

Elliot's body went rigid. Uchenna's eyes grew wide.

"What is it?" Uchenna whispered.

"Bobcat."

"Are you sure?" Uchenna's voice was barely a breath.

"No. Could be a bear."

"A bobcat or a bear?"

"Right. Or a tiger."

"Tigers live in the Pine Barrens?"

"If someone let one out of its cage, maybe."

"So you have no idea what it is, Elliot."

"That is correct."

The snarling continued. Now, though, it was mixed with whimpering. Uchenna scanned the forest. The sounds seemed to be coming from the deep brush to their right.

The class had gotten very far ahead of them on the path.

"Let's go check it out," Uchenna said.

"*What?*" Elliot hissed. *"Are you kidding? I'm fairly confident it's either a bobcat or a bear. My tiger theory was far-fetched, admittedly, but . . ."*

Uchenna wasn't listening. She checked to

make sure Professor Fauna and Miss Vole weren't looking. They were already around a bend and out of sight.

Uchenna stepped off the path, slid between two dense bushes, and disappeared.

Elliot stared after her, completely dumbfounded. *"Of course,"* he muttered to himself. *"I have one friend at my new school, and it turns out she's got a death wish."*

He waited.

He began to chew on a fingernail.

He looked down the path to see if someone was coming back to get them. He hoped they were.

They weren't.

He chewed his fingernail some more.

All of this took about three seconds.

And then a scream shattered the stillness of the woods.

CHAPTER SEVEN

Elliot stared at the dark bushes. There were about a hundred ways for Uchenna to die in there. In ninety-eight of them, rushing in after her wouldn't do any good. It would just get Elliot killed, too.

So, he stood there, legs trembling.

The bushes were dark and still. The class was far out of sight. He considered shouting for help. If he did, Miss Vole and Professor Fauna would come. They would help Uchenna.

Probably. Unless whatever was in there ate them, too.

Alternatively, he could faint. That would, at least, remove him from consciousness until this whole horrible situation was resolved.

Finally, he could run away, navigating the twisting paths of the Pine Barrens with his reasonably accurate mental map, locate the highway, and follow it home. He could beg his mother and grandmother not to send him back to this horrible school, with the terrifying professor of social studies and where his only friend had been eaten by a bear. Or a bobcat. Or, more improbably, a tiger.

Scream?

Faint?

Run away?

And then, to Elliot's total and utter shock, he found himself doing none of those things.

He found himself following Uchenna into the bushes.

He stumbled forward. Catbrier thorns caught his clothes; his curly hair got tangled in its branches. He pushed ahead—gasping at the sight of a poisonous pitcher plant—wondering what he was doing, and what possible force on earth could have sent him after this crazy girl into a thicket with a hungry predator.

And then Elliot's foot caught in a tangle of pine roots. He felt a moment of panic, his arms flailed, and he went tumbling, headfirst, through another catbrier bush and . . . *BAM!* onto his face.

He was lying on his belly in a small, sun-filled clearing.

He looked around.

Uchenna was crouched on one knee, apparently unscathed. But her mouth was hanging open, and her eyes were wider than headlights.

Elliot lay flat upon the ground. *"Uchenna,"* he whispered, *"what are you . . ."*

And then he stopped.

He saw it.

It was not a bear.

It was not a bobcat.

It was not a tiger.

It was, instead, the strangest-looking creature either child had ever seen.

CHAPTER EIGHT

It had a body like a tiny deer's.

But it had wings.

And claws on its front legs.

And hooves in the back.

And sharp teeth.

And it was blue. Except for its belly and its wings, which were red.

And a face that looked, more than anything, like a tiny dragon's.

Elliot would have been insanely terrified, except for the fact that it was rather small. About the size of a cat.

Also, it was completely caught in a tangle of pink ribbon.

"*Good gracious!*" Elliot muttered. "*What is that thing?*"

"*No idea,*" breathed Uchenna.

They watched the little creature. It was rolling around on the sunny ground, trying to escape the loops of ribbon that wound around its chest and neck.

"*Maybe we should help it,*" Uchenna said.

"*Absolutely not! Do not touch it, under any circumstances! Wild creatures can be incredibly dangerous!*"

The little creature continued to fight with the ribbon. The harder it fought, the tighter the ribbon seemed to constrict. After another moment, the animal fell still. Its tiny flank rose and fell, rose and fell. It was struggling to breathe.

"I think it's in more danger than we are," Uchenna said.

She moved toward the strange animal, dragging her knees across the sunny clearing.

"*Careful!*" Elliot hissed.

But Uchenna was purring. "Shhh . . . ," she purred. "Shhh . . ."

The animal caught sight of her. One of its large round eyes focused on her.

Uchenna inched forward.

The creature started to growl, deep in its throat.

"*Uchenna,*" Elliot whispered. "*This is a horrible idea.*"

But Uchenna just purred. "Shhh . . . Shhh . . ." And still her knees slid over the muddy turf. "Shhh . . . Shhh . . ." She reached out her hand. The little beast was still growling. She touched its forehead. Slowly, she ran her hand over the long ridge of its skull. "*It's soft,*" Uchenna whispered. "*And velvety. It's kinda nice.*"

"You're kidding."

Uchenna stroked the creature's head again and again. After a while, it stopped growling at her. Its eyelids, which came from the sides of its eyes, began to flutter. Its red wings curled up against its body. It exhaled through the two round nostrils at the end of its blue snout. Its body began to relax.

"*Okay,*" Uchenna whispered. "*Now come over here and take this stuff off it.*"

"What!?" Elliot cried.

The animal's eyes shot open.

"Shhh!" Uchenna hissed at Elliot. And then she started to purr again. "Shhh . . . Shhh . . ." She continued to stroke the creature's blue head.

After a moment, the little beast's eyelids closed once more. *"Now,"* Uchenna whispered. "Quietly *come over here and take this ribbon off.*"

"Fine," Elliot snapped. "But if I die, I'm suing you."

"Right. That makes sense."

Elliot, very unhappily, let his hands fall into the mud, and then he began crawling on all fours toward the creature. When he arrived, he breathed through his nose, set his chin, and then reached out for the ribbon that was wrapped around the animal's neck. It was twisted into a loop. He took hold of it. "Shhh," Uchenna murmured. Slowly, Elliot pulled the loop over the creature's head.

Suddenly, its eye opened.

"AHHH!" Elliot screamed. "It was a trap!"

"Shhh!" Uchenna hissed.

The little creature jumped up, the ribbon now around its jaw and over one eye.

Elliot and Uchenna fell backward. "It was a trap . . . ," Elliot mumbled. "It was a trap. . . ."

The beast growled at them, its one free eye round and furious.

"*It wasn't a trap!*" Uchenna hissed. "*You just scared it.*"

The animal tried to snap at them, but the ribbon held its mouth closed. Its claws dug into the earth.

"Shhh . . . ," Uchenna purred.

But the creature was done being soothed.

It was angry.

CHAPTER NINE

The little blue beast growled at Elliot and Uchenna, its claws scraping at the soft earth, the pink ribbon wrapped across its face.

It came closer to them. With each step, its small red wings flapped slowly.

Elliot and Uchenna scrambled backward. The creature tried to snap its jaws at them, but since it could barely open its mouth, its teeth just made little clicking sounds. Still, its claws were sharp, and if the pink ribbon came off, those teeth would draw blood. Lots of blood.

The creature stepped forward.

The children scooted back.

The creature stepped forward again.

The children scooted back again.

The creature stepped forward once more.

Uchenna scooted back.

Elliot did not. He was reaching into his pocket.

"What are you doing?" Uchenna whispered.

The little animal was getting uncomfortably close to Elliot. A few more steps and those claws would come into play.

"Are you hungry, Uchenna?" Elliot asked. "Want a snack?"

"What?" Uchenna demanded. *"Now?"*

"I'm hungry," said Elliot.

The sharp-toothed creature was no more than three feet away from Elliot. The ribbon hung from its face and trailed along the ground.

"And if I'm hungry," Elliot said, "that little guy is probably starving." He pulled the foil-wrapped almond bar from his pocket. He un-wrapped the foil. He dropped half of the bar onto the ground. He scooted away from it.

The creature stopped growling. It sniffed the air with its round nostrils. Then it put its nose on the ground and snuffled forward through the sun-light, its wings pulsing up and down with each step.

Elliot and Uchenna watched.

When the strange animal reached the piece of gooey almond bar, it sniffed it, and then tried to grab it with its mouth—but its jaws would not open far enough. It pushed the chunk of bar around with its nose, trying to figure out how to get its mouth around it. The creature was com-pletely ignoring the children now.

"Great job, Elliot! It's distracted! Let's go!" Uchenna whispered.

But Elliot said, "Nope. Now you need grab the ribbon." Elliot pointed at the pink trail of ribbon that hung off the creature's head.

Uchenna turned to her new friend. "Wait, now *you* want to help it?"

Elliot set his jaw. "Yeah. I guess I do."

Uchenna nodded. "Cool." Then she said, "Why don't you grab the ribbon?"

"Are you kidding? I'm terrified!"

Uchenna crept back to where Elliot was crouching.

The winged creature was trying to grab the bar with its blue lips.

Uchenna lunged forward and snatched the end of the ribbon farthest from the creature's face. The little beast squealed and pulled back. The ribbon went *pop*.

Uchenna held the ribbon in her hand. She

could see now that it was a balloon ribbon. Shreds of purple balloon clung to one end.

She also saw that the creature was free.

Free to use its jaws again.

CHAPTER TEN

The little beast growled at them, baring its tiny, sharp teeth.

"Huh. It doesn't seem any friendlier," Uchenna said.

"RUN!" cried Elliot.

The children turned, jumped to their feet, and sprinted for the path.

The creature leaped. They could hear its bat-like wings beating.

Elliot felt something sharp dig into his neck. He spun, crying out—

Thorns. Thorns had caught his bare skin. He yanked them away, leaving beads of blood. Meanwhile, Uchenna looked around. Where was the creature?

It was on the other side of the brambles. When Elliot screamed, he had dropped the rest of his almond bar. The strange blue animal pounced on it, like a cat hunting a mouse. It had

the bar in its jaws. Suddenly, it plopped down on its side—like a cat that had found a sunbeam. It held the almond bar in its claws and gnawed on it with the side of its mouth.

"Hey!" Elliot said. "It likes my mom's bar!"

They watched the blue creature roll around on the swampy, sunlit ground.

"It's kind of cute," Uchenna murmured.

"I wouldn't go that far."

The sun shone on its blue fur and red wings. It seemed to be . . . purring.

And then, Elliot remembered where they were—and where they were not. "We need to get back to the class!"

Uchenna agreed. "They're probably *really* far away by now."

"I wonder if Professor Freaky has noticed we're gone yet."

They locked eyes. They ran.

In the clearing, the little creature perked up its head and watched them go.

CHAPTER ELEVEN

The two children sprinted along the pine-needle-covered trail, under the spindly trees. The shadows flickered over their faces. The sun was high in the sky now, and the air was hot and still.

"Do you hear them?" Elliot panted.

"No. Come on! Run!" said Uchenna.

"I'm running as fast as I can!"

"Really? Oh."

Elliot frowned and pumped his arms harder. He started to catch up with Uchenna. "There you go!" she cried. Then she sped up. Elliot groaned.

They catapulted around a bend, Elliot right behind Uchenna—

SLAM!

Uchenna bounced and fell backward onto her rear end. Elliot came skidding to a halt.

They both looked up.

Professor Fauna towered over them. His hair stood on end. His black-and-white eyebrows and whiskers bristled. And his eyes—well, his eyes looked like *death*.

"*Palabrota!* Where have you been? What have you been doing?" The professor was not shouting. He was whispering. And his voice was trembling. Which was much more frightening than if he'd been shouting. "Do you know what is in this forest? Do you know how dangerous this place is? How deadly? What *secrets* lurk here?" His Adam's apple, which stuck out from his wrinkled neck,

went up and down. Suddenly, he turned away from them.

Elliot and Uchenna did not move as Professor Fauna started back down the path.

Without turning around, Professor Fauna said, "It would be unwise not to follow me."

Elliot and Uchenna were sure he was right.

Professor Fauna marched out ahead of them, his tweed suit plastered with dust and his leather shoes caked with mud. Elliot wrung his hands. Sweat prickled on the back of his neck. The forest felt colder, darker now. He *hated* getting in trouble.

Uchenna glanced into the trees to their right. Then she did it again.

"*What?*" Elliot whispered.

"*I don't know,*" Uchenna replied, her voice barely audible. "*I think there's something there.*"

A catbrier rustled. Then a blue jay took flight from it.

"It was just a bird," Elliot said.

Uchenna nodded. But she continued glancing over her shoulder into the trees.

When Miss Vole caught sight of Professor Fauna leading Elliot and Uchenna down the path, she hustled over to them with furious little steps. All the students saw this and immediately positioned their fingers over their ears.

But Miss Vole's voice dropped about four octaves. "I have never—been so afraid—in my life," she said. "Anything could have happened to you! You could have been attacked by a bear!"

Elliot nodded and let his head fall to his chest.

"Or had to fight a bobcat!"

Elliot's head snapped back up. "That's what I said!"

Miss Vole was in no mood to be interrupted. "Or been kidnapped by pirates!"

"Wait, are there still pirates—?" Uchenna began.

Miss Vole cut her off. "Or accidentally drunk poison from a pitcher plant!"

"How would we *accidentally*—?"

"Or been eaten by a tiger!"

Uchenna and Elliot looked at each other.

"If it escaped a cage somewhere," Miss Vole clarified.

Elliot turned to Uchenna. "See?!?" Uchenna rolled her eyes.

Their teacher raised a single finger. Both children fell silent. Their shoulders drooped. Their teacher sighed. "Sometimes, I think I should have stayed in the marines." Then she turned away from them.

Uchenna said, "You were in the marines?" But Miss Vole was done talking.

Uchenna felt something on the back of her neck. She turned and saw Professor Fauna glowering at her from under his dark brows.

CHAPTER TWELVE

The tour continued. Professor Fauna led the class through a stand of cool white cedars, and then up a hill. The pine trees were very short here, and sunlight warmed and dried the rocky ground.

At the top of the hill stood a ramshackle wooden house. The white cedar logs that made the walls were rotting, and red paint peeled off the windowsills. Many of the windows were broken or boarded over. Elliot thought it looked like

a set in a horror movie. Not that he'd ever seen a horror movie. But he imagined that's where they took place.

Miss Vole hurried up to the professor. "Professor Fauna, we are not going in that house, are we? That was decidedly *not* on the permission slips!"

"Miss Vole! Must you question everything I do?" The teacher's nerves were becoming frayed. "Of *course* we are going in that house."

"But it doesn't look safe!"

Professor Fauna smiled grimly and continued striding toward the run-down building. "Indeed. Danger is the greatest teacher." Uchenna's ears perked up. That was an interesting idea. Elliot, on the other hand, froze in place. Uchenna had to push him from behind to keep him moving forward.

Professor Fauna rapped with his big knuckles on the peeling red paint of the door.

A voice from inside called, "Hold on! Hold on! Hold on!"

Professor Fauna turned to the children. "In the Pine Barrens," he said, "it is typical to repeat things three times."

"Why?" someone asked.

"Because—" The professor raised his finger as if he were about to deliver a lecture. Then he let it fall. "Actually, I have no idea. People are different, all over the world. Also, they are the same. This is what makes the world such a wondrous and wonderful place. Wondrous, for the differences. Wonderful, for the sameness."

Just then, the door to the ramshackle house swung open. A thin, tiny woman stood in the doorway. She had large brown eyes and skin like newspapers that have been crumpled into balls and then smoothed out again. Her cheekbones were high and strong, her nose was straight and wide, and her hair was reddish-brown, but appeared to have the texture of Uchenna's. When she saw the professor, she smiled. "Oh, Dr. Fauna!" she cried, and she reached out her thin arms. The professor allowed himself to be hugged, though he didn't look very happy about it. "How are you, how are you, how are you?"

"I am very well, Dr. Thomas," the professor replied,

trying to escape her embrace without pushing the tiny woman over. "It is . . . ahem . . . a pleasure, as always." He slipped out from between her arms, straightened his tattered tweed suit, and then bowed to her. She laughed and bowed back. So he bowed again. She laughed some more and motioned the whole class inside.

CHAPTER THIRTEEN

They filed into a small room, which was very dark, since half the windows were boarded up. A flickering kerosene lamp sat atop a potbelly stove. A sagging bed sat in a corner. On second thought, maybe Elliot *had* seen a horror movie, one time, and it had definitely taken place right here. "Come in, come in, come in!" Dr. Thomas called, waving a spindly arm at the children. "Sit down, sit down, sit down!"

They all sat down in a big circle on the floor.

Dust lay an inch thick on the creaking floorboards. A spider crawled over the spot where Elliot had been planning to sit down. He shuddered and moved to the other side of Uchenna.

"I'm all ready for you!" Dr. Thomas said, and began passing out tiny mason jars with clear liquid in them. Elliot smelled it and wrinkled his nose. *Probably poison*, he thought. But the tiny doctor said, "It's sassafras tea! Not strictly legal, but it's never hurt anybody, as far as I know."

Not strictly legal? Elliot stared at the liquid. *In other words,* definitely *poison,* he told himself.

The professor raised his mason jar and said, "My young *amigos,* allow me to introduce you to Griselle Thomas. She is a very important woman. She is a keeper of history, a guardian of the land, and a protector of things that must remain unseen. . . ."

Uchenna and Elliot cocked eyebrows at each other.

"She will be our *woodjin,*" the professor went on. "Our guide to the Pine Barrens."

"Except I won't be hiking around with you," Dr. Thomas said, "'cause I'm too darn old." She raised her glass jar. "Bottoms up!"

Professor Fauna tipped his jar back and drained the sassafras tea. Miss Vole sniffed hers, smiled, and put it behind her. Elliot quickly did the same, as did most of the other children. But Uchenna drank her whole jar down.

Elliot stared at Uchenna. *"How does it taste?"*

"Weird," Uchenna replied. *"Like flat root beer."* She paused. *"I kind of like it. Can I have yours?"*

Elliot pushed his jar at her.

Professor Fauna began to speak. "Dr. Thomas lived in the Pine Barrens most of her life. Now she lives in Princeton, New Jersey, because the shopping is better."

Dr. Thomas laughed. "I live there because my daughter is a doctor at the university. But I was born and brought up in this house. My mother lived in this house, and her mother lived in this house, and her mother lived in this house."

"Yes, Dr. Thomas! Tell us about your amazing family!" Professor Fauna said.

Dr. Thomas nodded and smiled. "Well, my great-great-grandpa was of the Lenni-Lenapi Indian tribe. There're Irish folks in my background. French. I used to visit my Jewish cousins every summer, outside of Philadelphia. No idea *how* we were related, but everyone said we were." She laughed. "I kind of think of myself as a mix of every race, every people in New Jersey. I'm like a medley—a bunch of different songs, all flowing together," she concluded.

"That's what my daddy says about me!" Uchenna exclaimed. "Because my mom is from Lagos, in Nigeria. And my daddy is from New Orleans."

Dr. Thomas nodded. "So you're a medley, and I'm a medley—I guess we must be sisters!"

Uchenna said, "You're too old to be my sister."

Dr. Thomas suddenly stopped laughing. She crossed her thin arms and raised a threatening eyebrow.

Uchenna yelped, "Oh! Sorry!"

But Dr. Thomas had started laughing again.

CHAPTER FOURTEEN

The light from the kerosene lamp flickered over the faces of the people in the cabin. Elliot tried to fight off the spider that was now determined to crawl in the gaps between the floorboards he was sitting on—without actually touching the spider.

"Those mason jars you're drinking from—well, *some* of you are drinking from," Dr. Thomas said, eyeing Miss Vole, "the first one of those in history was made right here, in the Pine Barrens."

The old woman leaned her head back and smiled. "Yes, yes, yes, the Pine Barrens are a strange and wondrous place. Aren't many places like this in the whole world."

The children settled into more comfortable positions. It looked like Dr. Thomas was winding up to tell a story. She sounded like she knew how to tell a story, too. Children can always tell.

"For a long, long time, the Pine Barrens has been a place for medleys like me. And for people who don't quite fit in. The Lenni-Lenape tribe was here first, of course. Many were forced off their land by colonists, but some remained— they're still here, you know, keeping the traditions strong.

"Then, in the time of the American Revolution, there were people called Tories, who wanted America to be loyal to the king of England, and stay an English colony. They weren't real popular during the Revolution, so they came to hide here in the Pines.

"Around the same time, there came the Quakers. Quakers don't believe in fighting—ever, no matter what. I don't blame them. But some Quakers believed so much in the Revolution, and in America being free, that they went and fought the British anyway. Well, after the war, they weren't welcome at home, since they had fought. So they came to live here, too.

"Now can you imagine that? Quakers who wanted to fight for independence so much that they had to leave their homes, and Tories who loved the king so much they had to leave, too? And both of them, living side by side?

"Then there was the Underground Railroad. When slaves came north, escaping their chains, there used to be a saying: 'When you get to Jersey, don't stop until the pines are no taller than a man.' Any closer to Philadelphia and you were liable to get snatched by a slave hunter. You saw the little pine trees outside my house?"

The children nodded silently.

"Well, my great-grandfather got to those pygmy pines, and he stopped, and built this home. Out here, black people could live free. There are whole towns, not too far from this house, started by slaves who found their way to freedom.

"So you had American Indians and Tories and Quakers and escaped slaves—and pirates, too! Professor Fauna told you about the pirates, didn't he? He would have. He does love talking about those pirates. You had all these people, living here together in these pines. Now what does that sound like to you?"

"It sounds like a *mess*!" Miss Vole said.

"Ha!" Dr. Thomas slapped her knee. "You're darn right! You're darn right! You're darn right! It *was* a mess. And it was more than that. It was a melting pot, if you know what I mean."

Professor Fauna leaned forward and stroked his beard.

Dr. Thomas pointed a papery finger at the children. "You had all these rich men, Washington and Jefferson and all, running up and down the East Coast, saying they were fighting for a place where people could live free. But those Tories couldn't live free. The Lenni-Lenape couldn't live free. Those slaves *surely* couldn't."

Dr. Thomas sighed. "The wood for Thomas

Jefferson's desk, which he wrote the Declaration of Independence on, came from the Pine Barrens. Did you all know that?" The children shook their heads. "Course you didn't. The Founding Fathers thought they were inventing America. But *we* were the ones inventing America. And you know what America looks like? It looks like me." Dr. Thomas tapped her chest with her bony hand. "Look right here, children. It looks like me."

CHAPTER FIFTEEN

The small wooden house fell quiet. A few children shifted, and the floorboards beneath them creaked. Elliot had forgotten about the spider just long enough for it to crawl over his shirt and onto his neck. He tried frantically to flick it away.

Professor Fauna cleared his throat. "Dr. Thomas," he said, "would you mind, now, telling us about the Devil?"

"WHAT?" Miss Vole squealed. Everyone clapped their hands over their ears. Somewhere, a very old dog had a minor heart attack. "Professor Fauna! That is *not* an appropriate subject! In fact, this whole field trip has been inappropriate! I don't know *what* you were thinking, bringing these children to this place, but . . ."

"Miss Vole." Professor Fauna sighed. "I meant the Jersey Devil. The animal."

Miss Vole stopped speaking. "Oh." She paused. And then, very dismissively, she said, "But that's just a myth."

The professor fixed Miss Vole with a dark stare. "Children, your teacher is one of those ignorant people who believe that just because something is a myth, it cannot also be true. I have decided that you should not listen to your teacher."

The children gasped. Miss Vole tried to reply, but her mouth merely moved, and no sound came out.

The professor turned to the old doctor of the Pines. "Dr. Thomas, if you please."

The children leaned forward.

"My family," Dr. Thomas began, "has been full of doctors as long as anyone can remember. My mother was a doctor, and her mother was a doctor, and her mother before that. Now, in the old days, it wasn't easy to get training at a medical school as a woman from the Pines. We never had a lot of money, and we're mixed race, and everyone always expected a doctor to be a man. That's changing now, though not as fast as you'd think.

"Anyway, my great-great-great-great-great-grandmother, Beulah Thomas, was one of these self-taught woman doctors. She had a patient called Mrs. Leeds. Mrs. Leeds had twelve children. *Twelve!* Well, after Beulah delivered Mrs. Leeds's twelfth baby, Mrs. Leeds said, 'I won't be having any more children. I'd rather have the *devil* than have another child.' Well, she shouldn't have said that. Because less than a year later, she was giving birth again, and my great-great-great-great-great-grandmother was called, and that thirteenth baby wasn't a baby at all. It was a strange creature, and it went screeching out of Beulah's arms and straight through the window, leaving shattered glass all over Mrs. Leeds's floor."

The mouth of every child hung wide-open.

"Ever since then, the Jersey Devil roams these Pines."

"Tell us," Professor Fauna cut in, "what it looks like."

"Oh, they say the Jersey Devil's about the size of a deer. 'Bout the same shape, too. But it has wings, like a bat. It's got claws in front and hooves behind. And sharp teeth. Oh yes, and he's *blue*. A furry blue all over, with red wings."

Elliot and Uchenna stopped breathing.

The floorboards creaked as Dr. Thomas shifted and collected herself to continue. Before she could go on, Elliot very slowly raised his hand.

Uchenna hissed, *"Not now."*

But Dr. Thomas said, "Yes, darling?"

Elliot swallowed hard. Everyone was staring at him. He said, "Are you sure it's the size of a deer? Could it be . . . smaller than that?"

Dr. Thomas furrowed her brow and stuck out her chin.

"Well," Professor Fauna cut in, with his deep,

gravelly voice, "the story Dr. Thomas told is just that—a story."

"It doesn't exist!" Miss Vole exclaimed. "I knew it!" She sounded very relieved.

"Quite the contrary, Miss Vole," Professor Fauna replied. "*It* does not exist. *They* do. The story about Mrs. Leeds and her thirteenth child is poppycock, I am sure of it. But the Jersey Devil is a real animal. Not recognized by most scientists, perhaps. But phylum Chordata, class either Mammalia or Reptilia, superorder *perhaps* Dinosauria? Its social structure resembles that of mountain goats, where the males are solitary, and the females travel in small groups."

"Why do they call it a devil?" Elliot asked. He had dispensed with the formality of raising his hand now that Professor Fauna was speaking his language—the scientific study of animals.

Dr. Thomas said, "Well, parts of it look like a deer, like I said. But other parts look like a bat. Its fur is like a weasel's. And its colors are like a

bird's. In other words, it's kind of a medley. Like the people of the Pines. And for years and years, people didn't like medleys. They were scared of us. *That's* why they called it a devil." Dr. Thomas put her bony hands on the floorboards and leaned forward. "But you listen to me: The Jersey Devil is the most American creature that ever lived. The bald eagle shouldn't be on the dollar bill. No, no, no. The Jersey Devil should be. The Jersey Devil should be. The Jersey Devil should be."

CHAPTER SIXTEEN

Dr. Thomas stood by the door as the children filed out of the cottage. Most of the kids slid past her as quickly as they could, freaked out by her dark house and the story of the Jersey Devil.

But Uchenna stopped right in front of her and stuck out her hand. "It was nice meeting you," she said.

Dr. Thomas grinned down at the little girl. "Nice to meet you, too, sweetheart." They shook hands. Holding Dr. Thomas's thin hand was like holding a baby bird.

Professor Fauna pointed Miss Vole and the class toward the parking lot, and then hurried back to exchange a few hushed words with Griselle Thomas. As they spoke, they glanced toward the children. Elliot felt certain they were talking about him and Uchenna.

Once they were out of sight, Elliot murmured to Uchenna, "I noticed something kind of weird today."

"You noticed *one* weird thing today?"

"Well, a couple. But I'm talking about Dr. Thomas's ring. Did you see it?"

Uchenna shrugged and shook her head.

Elliot leaned closer to Uchenna. "Dr. Thomas was wearing a thick metal ring, with a unicorn on it."

"So?"

"Professor Fauna has the same ring."

Uchenna frowned. "Okay. That's a little

weird. But it's definitely *not* the weirdest thing that happened today."

"Fair enough. Another weird thing: I *also* have cousins outside of Philadelphia . . . who are *also* Jewish. . . ."

"Maybe you and Dr. Thomas are related!" exclaimed Uchenna.

Elliot thought about that for a minute. Then he said, "Do you think we should tell someone?"

"About you being related to Dr. Thomas?"

"No! About what we saw. The . . . you know . . ."

But before Uchenna could answer, they

arrived in the sun-drenched parking lot. Miss Vole instructed everyone to sit down on the dusty ground while she went to the bus to get their lunches.

"You two," she said to Elliot and Uchenna, "follow me."

She marched them to the big yellow bus, parked in the shade, where she began to lecture them. "I am shocked you two would be so utterly reckless! Especially you, Elliot! On your first day!" Elliot wanted to curl up into a ball of shame. "I thought of some more things that could have happened to you! What if you had fallen in the swamp? Or been attacked by a swarm of bees? Or even one of those—you know—Jersey Devils?"

Elliot and Uchenna both stared up at Miss Vole, unblinking.

Their teacher closed her eyes and took a deep breath through her nostrils, and then out of her mouth. It looked like something she'd learned in a yoga and meditation class. Or maybe in the marines. Then she said, "You two are going to eat your lunches on the bus. I know it's hot. I know it's uncomfortable. But maybe that'll give you a little taste of how I felt when you two went missing." She collected the other kids' lunches and left.

Elliot and Uchenna slouched to the back of the bus. Uchenna smacked each big green seat as she passed it, and then collapsed into the last one. Elliot plopped down beside her.

"Miss Vole is going to call our parents, I know it," Elliot mumbled.

"My dad is going to kill me. I am dead. One hundred percent dead."

"It's weird how adults always threaten to kill you when you do something dangerous and against the rules, right?" Elliot mumbled. "They're like, 'You almost died! So now *I'm* going to kill you!' It doesn't make any sense."

Uchenna sighed and gazed out the window.

"Elliot!" she said, sitting up. "Look!"

Elliot leaned over to look out the smudged school bus window. His eyes grew wider and wider. His mouth, slowly, fell open.

Half of a Jersey Devil was creeping through the dusty parking lot, toward the bus.

Yes. *Half.*

CHAPTER SEVENTEEN

They were looking out the window of the bus that faced away from where the class was having lunch. The sun was shimmering on the blue velvety fur of the small Jersey Devil they had encountered in the clearing—well, one *half* of it. One red wing, almost translucent in the sunlight, rose and fell with each step.

"What is going on?" Uchenna muttered.

Elliot just shook his head and stared.

The little creature veered right, and more of

it appeared. But then it came to the shadow of the school bus—and lost its head. Elliot shrieked. As it approached the bus, it disappeared entirely. Elliot and Uchenna heard a flapping of wings.

Then they shouted—there was a scratching, scrabbling sound on the school bus window.

"Help! Someone help!" Elliot cried.

Uchenna shielded him with her body. She was staring at the window. They could see the Jersey Devil's head and neck, illuminated by the slanting sunlight shining into the bus. Its head was turned sideways, and it was peering at them with a round, shocking eye. The bottom half of the creature's body was completely invisible.

"That is amazing . . . ," Uchenna murmured.

"It looks like it's invisible in the shade, but not in the sun. I wonder what the organic mechanism for—"

"Elliot!" Uchenna snapped. "What are we going to do?" The Jersey Devil's eye roved over them. "Should we let it in?"

"WHAT? NO!" Elliot shouted.

Uchenna shrugged. "I think he wants to come in." The creature's claws scrabbled at the window.

"Yeah, to *eat* us."

"I think he likes your almond bars better than he likes us. Do you have any more?"

"You've got to be kidding."

"Give me one."

"No."

"Fine." Uchenna stood up, gripped the clasps of the school bus window, and let it slide open.

"Uchenna!" Elliot cried.

But the Jersey Devil was already scrambling over the window and into the bus. As its body passed through the bar of sunlight, it became visible, but as soon as it dropped into the shade of the bus, it completely disappeared again. That is, until it totally reappeared, sitting on Uchenna's half of the bus seat. She stood against the window, staring. Elliot was sitting right next to the Jersey Devil.

"Huh. It seems it can *choose* to be invisible in the shade, but not in the sun," Elliot mused. "Perhaps some of the melanin it produces doesn't reflect light, but rather—"

"Elliot!" Uchenna said. "Do you have any more of those bars or not?"

Elliot was about to respond—when the doors to the bus opened, and the rest of the class came pouring in.

CHAPTER EIGHTEEN

"Quick! Hide him!" Uchenna hissed.

Just as she said it, though, the Jersey Devil disappeared.

Elliot and Uchenna blinked. The other children were flooding down the aisle, plopping into their big green seats, chattering and shouting like any group of kids after lunch.

Slowly, Uchenna reached out her hand. She jerked it back. *"He's still there . . . ,"* she whispered.

Elliot reached out his hand—and then re-coiled in horror. "I think I just touched its eye-ball . . . ," he whimpered, wiping his hands on his pants.

Then there was the sound of something hitting the steel floor of the bus. Uchenna and Elliot peered into the dark space under their seat. Elliot's lunch bag appeared to be opening itself.

"What are you guys doing?"

Elliot and Uchenna shot up.

A girl with black eyeliner and black finger-nails was leaning over the back of the seat in front of them.

"Nothing!" they both answered at once.

The girl said, "*That* wasn't suspicious." Elliot and Uchenna both stared at her, unspeaking.

The girl shrugged. "Whatever." Then she said, "I thought Miss Vole was going to kill you."

Elliot brightened. "Isn't it funny how—" But the girl had already turned around and sat down again.

"Okay," Uchenna whispered. "Don't move." Very slowly, she looked under their seat. She sat back up.

"Well?" Elliot asked, as casually as he could. His legs were trembling.

"So, is there another almond bar in your lunch bag?"

"Yes, in fact—"

"Not anymore."

Elliot sighed. He looked under the seat. There were raisins everywhere. "That must have been one of my grandma's," he said.

"Yeah," agreed Uchenna. "I guess he doesn't like raisins."

"Why do you keep calling it 'he'? Did you see its personal anatomy?"

"Its *what?*"

"You know . . ." Elliot blushed. "Its . . . *personal . . . anatomy.*"

"Oh, you mean between its legs?" Uchenna said. Elliot blushed even harder. Uchenna didn't seem to notice. "No. It just looks like a boy to me."

The bus driver started up the motor, his pipe clamped between his teeth. Professor Fauna was walking down the aisle, checking that all the children had fastened their seat belts. Miss Vole was sitting at the front of the bus, looking like she was trying to avoid having a nervous breakdown.

The professor came even with Elliot and Uchenna's seat. He glared at them. His crazy eyebrows bristled. He sniffed.

The children smiled up at him innocently.

He turned around and made his way to the front of the bus. Elliot put his head in his hands.

The bus turned out of the parking lot.

An invisible Jersey Devil started eating Elliot's tuna fish sandwich.

CHAPTER NINETEEN

For the rest of the bus ride, the Jersey Devil made his way through Elliot's lunch, and then moved on to Uchenna's, while the two children whispered furiously to each other about what they should do.

Uchenna suggested helping the creature crawl back out the window.

"Everyone would see him. And then he would just fall into traffic," Elliot replied.

"He wouldn't fall. He can fly!"

"We know he can jump. Can he fly?"

"Well, he has wings."

"Yeah, so do chickens. You wanna toss the Jersey Devil into traffic and hope he uses his wings better than a chicken?"

"Well, no . . ."

The bus rumbled by the towering smokestacks of the Schmoke brothers' power plant, off the exit ramp, and into the school parking lot. The brakes screamed, the big yellow bus rocked forward and then back. Miss Vole rose to her feet—shakily—and said, "Now, children, go back to the classroom quietly, please. There's just half an hour before dismissa—" They didn't let her finish. The children burst from their seats and shoved past her off the bus. Miss Vole looked like she was about ready to quit. And it wasn't even the end of September.

Meanwhile, Elliot and Uchenna began whispering furiously.

"How do we get him off the bus?"

"He's invisible! Just carry him!"

"I'm not carrying him!" This was Elliot.

"Then let's put him in a backpack."

"That's a terrible idea!"

"Do you have a better one?"

"No . . . but he's not going in my *backpack!"*

Uchenna glared at Elliot. She looked under the seat. The Jersey Devil was nowhere to be seen.

Elliot leaned down beside Uchenna. He held very still. At last, he murmured, "Listen . . ." They heard a quiet whistling of breath, in and out, in and out. "I think he's asleep."

Uchenna took her books from her backpack and handed them to Elliot. Then, very gently, she reached out and touched the soft coat of the Jersey Devil. She found his side and slid her fingers down under it, until they were under his belly. The Jersey Devil snorted. Then Uchenna lifted the little creature and lowered him into her backpack.

Suddenly, there he was, staring at them, eyes

open. Elliot and Uchenna nearly leaped out of their seat.

The Jersey Devil reached out his long tongue—it was as blue as his body. Elliot recoiled in horror. Uchenna froze. The Jersey Devil licked Uchenna's hand.

Then he curled up in the backpack, closed his eyes, and disappeared again.

Uchenna was trembling, but she zipped her bag and hefted it onto her shoulder. Elliot picked up his own backpack—which was now twice as heavy, since it contained Uchenna's books as well. They made their way to the front of the bus.

Professor Fauna was waiting.

He rose from his seat as they approached. He glared down from his full, towering height, his eyes like spotlights under his mad, bushy eyebrows. The children stopped, like travelers at the foot of a cliff, and peered up.

"Well?" he intoned, in his rich bass voice. "Do you children have something you want to tell me?"

Elliot's hands grew damp.

Uchenna bit her lip. "Like . . . what?"

Professor Fauna's eyebrows crawled up his forehead like two hairy caterpillars.

"Oh," Uchenna said. "Right. We're sorry we got lost."

Fauna eyed her, not moving from the narrow bus aisle.

"Yes," Elliot added, "very sorry."

Still, the professor did not move. His dark eyes roved over them suspiciously.

And then he stepped aside.

"Remember, children, secrets can be dangerous."

Without missing a beat, Uchenna replied, "But danger is the greatest teacher."

The professor frowned at her. His black eyes looked like pits. "Unless," he said, "it kills you."

As they walked away from the bus, Elliot leaned over to Uchenna. "He actually has a torture chamber under the school?"

From the side of her mouth, Uchenna muttered, "That's what they say."

"I believe it."

CHAPTER TWENTY

U chenna held her backpack close to her chest for the remaining twenty minutes of the school day. When the bell rang, she and Elliot walked out of the front door of the elementary school, down the steep steps, and onto the street.

"Is your mom picking you up? Or your grandma?" Uchenna asked.

"Neither. They said I could walk home. Even though it's my first day."

"Some first day." Uchenna sighed.

"Yeah. If the whole year is like this," Elliot agreed, "I don't think I'll survive."

They walked side by side. Uchenna, it turned out, lived just one street away from Elliot.

"How's Jersey?" Elliot asked.

"Who?"

"Jersey, the Jersey Devil."

"That's the least creative name I've ever heard."

Elliot shrugged. "Yeah, but you have to admit, he's kind of cute."

"Who wants cute? Let's call him something awesome, like Bonechewer."

Elliot frowned.

"Bloodguzzler?"

Elliot's frown deepened.

"Bloodguzzler, Destroyer of Worlds?"

"Absolutely not."

"Bonechewer then," Uchenna said. She began to shout-sing:

"*Bonechewer! Bonechewer!*
He is from the swamp! Not the sewer!
Bonechewer! Bonechewer!
RRRRAHHHHHHHHHR!"

Uchenna did an extended drum solo in the air.

"You know," Elliot said, "Bonechewer also rhymes with *manure*. In case that helps you with the second verse."

Uchenna glared at him.

She zipped open her pack. The sun fell directly into the bag. The little Jersey Devil blinked up at the children.

Cautiously, Elliot reached in and touched the little creature's head. He closed his eyes. Elliot stroked his bony skull. A gurgling sound came from his throat.

"He's purring," Uchenna said. Some kids were walking toward them. She zipped up the backpack and they walked on.

CHAPTER TWENTY-ONE

Elliot and Uchenna approached a small park. A man was making balloon animals for a group of young children. He had a number of larger balloons bobbing behind his head.

"I want a unicorn!" one of the kids shouted.

The balloon-maker rubbed his unshaven chin. "Yeah, I can't make a unicorn. How about a snake? I can make snakes pretty good."

"A unicorn!"

"How about two snakes twisted together? I can do that."

"A unicorn!" the child shouted.

"A unicorn . . . a unicorn . . . ," the man muttered. Then his eyes brightened. "What about a unicorn horn? I can make a unicorn horn!"

The child clapped happily. The balloon man looked very relieved.

Elliot and Uchenna stopped to watch. In hushed tones, Elliot asked, "So, what are we going to do with Jersey?"

"Bonechewer? I say we take him to the forest. Let him go," Uchenna suggested.

"But he doesn't live anywhere near here! You can't just let him go in some random forest!"

"Why not?"

"That'd be like taking you to some small town in Mongolia, dropping you off, and saying, 'This looks like where you come from.' That's not called letting him go, that's called *kidnapping*."

THE CREATURE OF THE PINES

"Fine," Uchenna said. "Let's check on him again."

"We just checked on him thirty seconds ago."

"Yeah, but I . . . I kind of like him."

Elliot gave Uchenna a disapproving look. "We are *not* keeping him. That would be unethical and dangerous. Not to mention a logistical nightmare."

"What's logistical?" Uchenna asked absently as she unzipped her pack.

The little Jersey Devil stuck his head up out of the bag. He looked at them with one eye, and then turned his head and looked at them with the other. Then, his body tensed.

"What's wrong with him?" Elliot whispered.

"I don't know. Does he see something?"

"Is he afraid?"

The Jersey Devil started to growl.

"Oh no," Elliot murmured.

Suddenly, Uchenna stumbled back because the Jersey Devil had leaped out of the pack, down onto the sidewalk, and bounded toward the man with the balloons. The sunlight was dappled by the trees of the small park, and the Jersey Devil appeared and disappeared with every patch of shade and sunlight. Elliot and Uchenna stared in horror. No one had noticed the little blue creature with red wings. Yet.

And then, the Jersey Devil leaped—directly for a large pink balloon that hovered behind the balloon man's head. The creature passed through shade, and then sunlight. When the sunlight hit him, he was right next to the balloon man's face.

The man screamed. The Jersey Devil crashed into the large pink balloon. It popped. The Devil hit the ground and scampered away, into the park.

"I am developing a theory that Jersey Devils are obsessed with balloons," Elliot stated as the balloon man continued screaming and the little children laughed and clapped and demanded he make another disappearing deer-dragon balloon and their parents continued to check their phones.

"That's an interesting theory," Uchenna replied. "I have another one: We need to catch him. Now."

CHAPTER TWENTY-TWO

Elliot and Uchenna sprinted through the park. A flash of blue appeared between two trees. "There he is!" Uchenna shouted. But instantly he was gone again.

The park was small, and soon they'd searched the whole thing.

"Where is he?" Uchenna panted.

"No idea." Elliot heaved, bending over, his hands on his knees.

Uchenna looked around. "We can't let him wander all over town. He could be hit by a car. Or bite someone."

"And," Elliot added, still heaving, his hands still on his knees, "our balloons are all in mortal danger."

Elliot and Uchenna started walking again. They scoured the edge of the park, but the Jersey Devil was nowhere to be seen.

"This is surreal," Elliot muttered as Uchenna checked under a bench. "Jersey Devils aren't supposed to *be*. They're imaginary. Mythical."

"This one ate your snack bars," Uchenna said, getting up, brushing off her pants, and then peering into a trash can.

"He's not supposed to exist. And yet, I'm really, *really* worried about him."

Uchenna looked up from the trash can. "I know."

"What if he dies?" Elliot said. "What if he's

run over by a truck because we brought him here and then let him escape? That would be horrible. *Horrible.*" Elliot gripped his stomach and sat down on the bench. "I think I'm going to be sick."

Uchenna walked to the corner, checking under every bench, looking in every trash can, peering over the park fence, gazing across the street. Every time a car zoomed by, she shuddered.

The stoplight turned red, and a small, beat-up blue car came to a stop right beside Uchenna. She glanced at it—and then nearly jumped out of her shoes.

Professor Fauna was inside the car. He was muttering furiously to himself.

Uchenna glanced back at Elliot, who was doubled over on his bench. She looked at Professor Fauna, muttering in his car. She looked at the stoplight. Still red.

She stepped off the curb and into the street.

She knocked on the window of the car.

The professor turned. His huge eyebrows crawled up his forehead.

"Professor Fauna," Uchenna said, "we need your help."

CHAPTER TWENTY-THREE

Professor Fauna stared at Uchenna, standing in the street, next to his car. He mouthed something that looked like, *"What?"*

"We need your help!" Uchenna said more loudly.

Back on his bench, Elliot looked up. He squinted at Uchenna. Who was she talking to in that beat-up Ford Pinto?

Professor Fauna leaned over and cranked

down the window. Music blared from his tinny radio. *"Upside, inside out, she's livin' la vida loca . . . ,"* the singer sang. So he hadn't been muttering. He'd been singing along.

"Is everything okay, Uchenna?" he shouted. The music was very loud.

"No!" she said. "We need your help!"

"We? Who is we?"

Behind them, a horn blared. The professor looked up. The light was green.

"Elliot and I. We have something to tell you."

Professor Fauna pulled up the car's parking brake, shut off the engine, undid his seat belt, and was out of the Pinto—all within a second and a half.

The driver of the car behind him leaned on his horn again.

"Palabra mala!" Professor Fauna shouted. "Can't you see I'm talking to a student!? Go around! Go around, you fool!" He waved his arms

at the car. The driver continued to honk. Fauna threw his arms up in the air and stepped up onto the sidewalk, leaving his car parked in the middle of the street.

Elliot was watching all of this in horror. What was Uchenna doing? He hurried from his bench over to Uchenna and the professor. "What's going on?" he demanded.

"This is what I would like to know!" Professor Fauna replied. His eyebrows looked like two great lightning bolts, arched either with fury or with worry. It was hard to tell. "What is happening? Why are you banging on my window?"

Uchenna said, "Professor, Elliot and I have something to tell you."

"What?" said Fauna.

"What!?" said Elliot.

"We do. Elliot, tell him."

Fauna looked meaningfully at the pale

boy with the curly hair. Elliot stammered out,
"I—there—we—but—not—"

Fauna turned to Uchenna, "This boy has apparently lost the power of speech. You tell me!"

"We brought a Jersey Devil back from the Pine Barrens," Uchenna said. "And then we lost him."

Professor Fauna fell down on the pavement.

In the street, car horns blared.

CHAPTER TWENTY-FOUR

"What are you saying? Explain it to me! Everything!" Professor Fauna was sitting on a bench. He had fainted, and Elliot and Uchenna revived him by patting his big, hairy cheeks. Now they were fanning him with their hands. "Stop it! I have recovered! Explain yourselves!"

Elliot shot Uchenna a look that plainly said, "This was your idea. *You* tell him."

So Uchenna took a deep breath. "When we were in the Pine Barrens, we heard something.

Something strange. Like an animal. So we followed the sound—"

"*You* followed the sound!" Elliot cut in. "I followed you, because I heard you scream, and I thought you were in trouble, even though the chances were slim that I could help you, and high that I would lose my very life!"

Fauna squinted at Elliot, and then turned to Uchenna. "Does he always talk this way? Like a character in an old book?"

"Sometimes," said Uchenna. "Goes in and out. Anyway, we came to a clearing, and there was this . . . this little . . . Jersey Devil."

"It matched Dr. Thomas's descriptions in every particular," Elliot agreed. "Except that he was smaller."

"Amazing." Fauna sighed. "Never have I seen one, though the evidence was strong that they existed. What happened next? You did not touch him, did you?"

"Uh . . . ," said Uchenna.

"Uh . . . ," said Elliot.

"Because if you touched him, he may never return to the wild. At least, you have not fed him, right? Feeding him would be irreversible. He would *never* go back to his home!"

"Uh . . ."

"Uh . . ."

Professor Fauna's face contorted with horror. "You *fed* him?"

The children looked at each other. Then they both nodded.

"Palabrota indecible!" Professor Fauna grabbed his beard and pulled at it. "How did this happen?"

Uchenna told him. "He was being choked by an old balloon ribbon. We saved him."

"And then he was going to bite us," Elliot added. "So we fed him an almond bar. No raisins."

"He likes almonds."

"He doesn't like raisins. We found that out later."

Professor Fauna covered his face with his big hands. He muttered, "What happened next?"

"Well," Uchenna said, "he followed us onto the school bus, and then all the kids got on. And then the bus drove away. So we put him into my backpack."

"You didn't!"

"Yeah, we kept him in there for a while. He fell asleep. He's pretty cute."

Professor Fauna was staring at the children with a mixture of awe and horror.

"And then, when we were walking through this park, we opened the backpack to check on him, and he escaped and ran away."

"He saw a balloon," Elliot added. "He seems to have a homicidal obsession with balloons. Otherwise, he's pretty nice."

"So he is loose? In town?" Fauna groaned.

"Yeah, and he's hard to find, because he can turn invisible in the shade."

Fauna's eyes grew even wider. "Invisible . . . Of course! That explains why the species has been so hard to document. . . ." He stood up suddenly. "But we must find him! At once! He is in great danger!"

"We know. He could be hit by a car," Uchenna said.

"Or fall down a drain," Elliot cut in. "Or get

attacked by a dog. Or scooped up by a large owl. Or seen by a reporter, who would report on him, and then the whole town would be besieged by the media, and they'd start a huge hunt, and—"

"Elliot!" Uchenna snapped.

"Sorry. I had some time to come up with new things to worry about."

Professor Fauna was staring across the street. "There is something in this town much worse than all that, children. *Much* worse."

CHAPTER TWENTY-FIVE

Professor Fauna, Uchenna, and Elliot started walking. A tow truck was hitching up Fauna's blue Pinto in order to take it to the pound.

"Uh, Professor, don't you want to stop them?" Elliot said, gesturing at the truck.

Fauna waved his hand dismissively. "Happens to me all the time. Besides, we have far more important things to worry about!"

Across the street from the park was a neighborhood with all of the biggest houses in town.

Professor Fauna led the children there. As they walked past, they saw homes with dozens of windows and large garages. The small roads between the houses were quiet and empty of traffic. They had names like Pleasant Meadows and Waterfall Junction, even though there were no meadows or waterfalls anywhere nearby.

"We must think, children," Fauna said. "What do we know about the Jersey Devil that might help us find it?"

"He likes almonds," said Uchenna.

"And not raisins," said Elliot.

"Right. So if we see an almond-processing factory, we will go inside. If we see a raisin-boxing facility, we will not go in. Very helpful, children."

"Are you being sarcastic?" Elliot asked. "I don't know you very well, so—"

"Yes, I was being sarcastic! Keep thinking!"

"Well, we know his habitat," said Elliot. "He comes from the Pine Barrens."

"Ah! Now you are using that slightly over-large head of yours!"

Elliot turned to Uchenna. "Do I have a big head?"

She looked at it for a minute. "A little bit?"

Elliot looked pained.

Fauna was still talking: "So we must seek a habitat that is similar to the Pine Barrens. The Jersey Devil is likely to have fled there."

"Someplace dry," Uchenna said, "and, well, piney . . ."

"Wait!" Elliot cut in. "We didn't find him in the dry, piney part. We found him just outside the swamp."

"Ah!" Fauna exclaimed. "Now your big head is working extra time!"

"You mean *overtime*?"

"Whatever. So we must seek him in a wet, moist area. Somewhere rich with plant life, I would guess. Green and warm."

"Like, there?" Uchenna asked, pointing.

They all turned. They were passing by the largest mansion in town. It was three stories tall, as wide as a school, and made entirely of gray stone. Great iron gates barred the drive. On top of each gate was a huge golden *S*. On one side of the mansion stood an enormous greenhouse. Fronds of ferns and canopies of tropical trees pressed up against the glass.

"No," said Professor Fauna. "Not *like* there." He pointed.

High up in the glass facade of the greenhouse, in a bright ray of sunlight, a little blue creature was climbing through an open window.

"*Exactly* there."

CHAPTER TWENTY-SIX

"Shouldn't we just ask the owners if we can go in and get him?" Elliot said as Professor Fauna tried to hoist Uchenna over the huge iron fence. They were in the shadow of the big stone wall that ran along the edge of the property.

"What would we say?" Uchenna replied, gripping the iron bars and hauling herself higher. "We lost a mythical creature in your greenhouse? Can we go get him?"

"We could say we lost our cat."

"Our *blue* cat? With *wings*?"

Fauna was huffing and wheezing under Uchenna's weight. "It is . . . out of . . . the question. . . ." He staggered a little. "I have . . . knowledge of . . . the owners . . . of this place. . . ."

Uchenna got a leg over the top of the fence, steadied herself, brought her other leg over, and then climbed down to the ground on the other side. Fauna sighed heavily, withdrew a red handkerchief from his tweed jacket, and mopped his brow. "They are *not* to be trusted. Under any circumstances."

"Who are they?" Elliot asked. Uchenna ran along the inside of the fence to a small iron door. Glancing once toward the house, she unlatched the gate from the inside and let Elliot and Professor Fauna into the grounds.

"Come," said Fauna. "I will tell you as we go. But stay low. And be quiet." They pressed themselves into the shade of the great stone wall and slunk along it. "This is the mansion of the

Schmoke brothers, the owners of Schmoke Industries." He turned to the children. His face was dark and angry. "They are never, *ever* to be trusted," Fauna said. "Come."

After a minute or so, they came to the corner of the greenhouse. There was a door with a big shiny handle. Fauna reached out, pressed the handle down, and pushed the door open.

"For being such untrustworthy industrialists," Elliot said, "their security apparatus is pretty pathetic."

"Oh no," said Fauna. "I am certain that we have all been caught on camera already. I assume their house is built like a poisonous pitcher plant. Getting in is easy. Getting out is not."

CHAPTER TWENTY-SEVEN

Elliot would have turned around right then, but Uchenna had already slipped past the professor, into the greenhouse. Fauna was right behind her.

Elliot paused to consider. Brand-new friend. Terrifying teacher. Mythical animal. Breaking and entering. First day at a new school.

Well, at least it was educational.

As he grabbed the door to follow the professor, he noticed that the hinges were reinforced with heavy-duty springs. *Why would you spring-load a door?* Elliot wondered. He let it close—but stopped it just before the latch caught. He slid his backpack from his shoulders and propped the door open, just in case.

The air was thick and wet inside the greenhouse. They followed a carefully manicured stone path. On either side, enormous and strange vegetation hung over their heads. There were purple orchids with yellow tendrils that zigzagged like lightning bolts. There was a flower that was at least three feet wide and appeared to be covered in armor. There were Venus flytraps large enough to catch a small bird.

"Children," Fauna whispered, *"these are some of the rarest plants in the world."*

A path branched to the left, toward the center of the greenhouse. Uchenna took it. The plants grew stranger. There was an enormous lump of blue-green moss. A clear tube had been stuck into its side, and bluish liquid oozed down the tube

and into a beaker marked ELIXIR 1525. Nearby, a
pot with green water and lily pads stood on an
electric hot plate. The temperature dial was set just
shy of 212 degrees Fahrenheit. Fauna stopped to
investigate it. "This is fascinating!" he murmured.

"Professor, please focus," Elliot said.

"But you see—"

Just then, somewhere in the greenhouse, a door
opened. They all froze. Crisp footfalls on stone.

Uchenna grabbed the professor's hand and
yanked him off the path, into the dense, hanging tendrils of a small tree. Elliot stood exactly
where he was, unable to move a muscle. Uchenna
grabbed him by the shirt and pulled him next to
Fauna. They waited.

The clicking footsteps grew louder. And louder.
And louder. Uchenna was breathing hard. Fauna
was breathing harder. Elliot wasn't breathing at all.

Then, through the tendrils, they could see him. He was clearly a butler—he wore a black, pressed suit, white gloves, and a sneer of disapproval. He examined the temperature on the electric burner. Then he measured the level of blue liquid in the beaker. He took off one glove, finger by finger, and then plunged his pinkie into the blue-green moss. It came out orange. He nodded.

The butler was no more than a foot from Elliot, which made the boy's entire body quiver.

Uchenna glanced at her new friend, and then had to clap a hand over her mouth to stop herself from screaming. The hanging tendrils of the tree were entangling themselves with Elliot's hair. Uchenna reached up and grabbed her own head. Thin branches were braiding themselves into her black twists. She looked back at the professor. The tendrils had woven themselves into his beard, his hair, and even his long eyebrows. He was totally still, staring at Uchenna, looking terrified.

Uchenna held up one finger. Elliot and Fauna nodded. The footsteps receded. Finally, the butler was entirely out of earshot. Uchenna grabbed the tendrils on top of her head and tore at them. They would not break. She wrenched her head to the left and right. No use. They were as strong as iron.

Then she noticed Professor Fauna, running his fingers up and down the trunk of the tree, as if he were tickling it. To her great surprise, the tree's tendrils seemed to relax, before curling up and out of reach. They were free.

"*Go!*" Fauna whispered, and they all dashed out from under the tree and back onto the path.

"Did you just *tickle* that tree?" Elliot demanded.

"After a brief examination," Fauna explained, "I realized that it is an *Ailanthus humorous*." He shrugged. "It just likes to cuddle. But if it gets too—how do you say? Touchy-feely?—tickling usually does the trick."

And then, the clicking sound of fine shoes on composite stone grew louder again. They spun around.

The butler was walking toward them down the middle of the path, wearing only one glove, muttering to himself. "Must have left it by the moss, blast it. Come on, Phipps! Focus! You know the masters don't tolerate—" He looked up and stopped. His mouth fell open.

And then he began to scream.

CHAPTER TWENTY-EIGHT

"INTRUDERS!" the butler screamed at the top of his lungs. "INTRUDERS!" He started for Uchenna, who was closest, but Professor Fauna stepped in front of her and pulled himself up to his towering height. This apparently made the butler change his mind. He turned around and ran in the opposite direction.

"We must find that Jersey Devil! Now!" said the professor.

"I think I know where he is!" said Elliot. "Come on!"

Just then, a loud alarm sounded. Doors and windows began slamming shut. Elliot started running back the way they'd come. The alarm was blaring in his ears. He skidded to a stop in front of the giant Venus flytraps.

"Here!"

"What?" said Uchenna.

"Where?" said Professor Fauna.

"Look at the ground!" Elliot said.

"Why?"

"Flytraps eat insects!"

"So what?"

"Why do you think they do that?"

"Can we abandon the Socratic method, if you please?!" Professor Fauna cried.

"Because they grow in soil that's low in nitrogen. Just like pitcher plants!"

Uchenna's eyes lit up. "It's his habitat!"

Elliot peered past the flytraps. "Look, there

are pitcher plants back there, deep in the shade! I knew it!"

"But I don't see the Jersey Devil," said the professor. "Is he here?"

"I don't know," said Elliot.

"Can we lure him to us?" Uchenna asked. "Do you have another snack bar?" Elliot reached in his pockets, and then shook his head.

Under the sound of the alarm, they heard voices. "This way, sirs! They were over here!"

"Out of the way, Phipps!"

"Yes, one side! One side, I say!"

At the end of the path on which they stood, there appeared two men. They were both wearing bathrobes—one pastel green, one baby blue. Each bathrobe was monogrammed, one with ES and, the other, MS. One man was tall and fit. The other was short and toad-like. Both had thinning brown hair on the top of their shiny heads. And both were very, very rich. You could see it in their faces.

"Milton!" said the short, toad-like man. "It's—"

"I know who it is, Edmund!" replied the tall one.

Fauna turned to the two children. His face was more severe than they had ever seen. He spoke in a strained whisper. "Listen to me. You must run. Now."

"But—" Uchenna began.

"Your cat can look after itself," Fauna growled between clenched jaws. He pushed the children behind him and turned to face the Schmoke brothers.

Elliot tried to yank Uchenna toward the door, but Uchenna did not move. "My cat?" she said.

The professor did not reply. He was glaring at the two billionaires.

Milton Schmoke, on the other hand, was smiling. His hands were buried in the pockets of his bathrobe. "Her . . . *cat*, Professor?"

"Hmm . . . ," purred Edmund. "Do you think it's a *cat*, Milton?"

Fauna, Elliot, and Uchenna all took a step back.

"Maybe," said Milton. His eyes twinkled like cut sapphires above his chiseled cheekbones. "Or maybe it's something more *interesting* than a cat."

"Yes," said Edmund. His eyes twinkled like cut emeralds above lumps of fat. "More interesting and *rarer*."

"Oh, we do like rare things," said Milton.

"Indeed, we do," agreed Edmund.

"Is there something rare in our greenhouse, Professor?" Edmund said.

"Besides our collection of one-of-a-kind *flora*, of course," added Milton.

Professor Fauna cleared his throat. "Nothing rarer than a calico cat," he replied stiffly.

Which is when Elliot screamed. Phipps, the butler, had crept around behind them, and at that instant, he grabbed Elliot's arms. "I have him, sirs! I have the boy!"

"Thataway, Phipps!" Milton bellowed. "Don't let him go!" He advanced on Fauna, who raised his fists in a comical interpretation of a fighter's posture.

"I won't, sirs!" the butler yelled. "I have him very tightly—AHGHGH!"

Everyone turned to look at the butler. Attached to Phipps's face was a small blue body, with red wings beating frantically.

"OH, THERE'S SOME-THING ON MY FACE! THERE'S SOMETHING ON MY FACE! WHAT SHALL I DO, SIRS? WHAT SHALL I DO?"

"Grab it, Phipps! Grab it!" Edmund bellowed.

But he didn't have time to grab it, because Uchenna spun and punched Phipps in the stomach. She was only a kid, so she couldn't punch *very* hard. But she did double Phipps over. Elliot slid his hands under the Jersey Devil's forelegs. "Come here, Jersey," he murmured. The Jersey Devil turned around, held on to Elliot's shirt with his two front claws, and licked his face.

"This way!" Uchenna shouted, and she ran past Phipps, the butler, who was on his knees, patting his face and whimpering softly.

Elliot followed Uchenna.

But Fauna hung back.

He stuck out a finger at the Schmoke brothers. "You stay away from me, and you stay away from those children."

"You're in *our* house!" Milton protested.

"Quite right! We have every right to subdue and execute you!" Edmund agreed.

"Well, not every *legal* right . . . ," Milton said.

But Fauna was already halfway down the path, following the children. The alarm still blared in the distance.

Fauna found Elliot and Uchenna at the door they'd come through. It was trying to close, slamming shut on Elliot's backpack again and again and again, as a red light flashed overhead.

"Put him in here!" Uchenna barked at Elliot, turning her pack around to her stomach and holding it open. Elliot dropped the Jersey Devil inside and zipped it closed. They darted through the door as it opened, and then tried to slam on Elliot's backpack again. Fauna, bringing up the rear, scooped up Elliot's backpack as he went by. And then they were running across the Schmoke brothers' grounds, through the small iron gate, and down the sunny sidewalk.

They sprinted around a corner and for another block. Finally, they slowed to a trot, and then a walk. They were all panting heavily.

"We got . . . away . . . ," Elliot said, heaving. "Their security apparatus . . . stinks. . . ."

But Fauna, between gasps of air, shook his head. "My guess is . . . they let us . . . let us go. . . ."

"Why would . . . they do that?" Uchenna asked.

"We have . . . a history," Fauna said, wheezing.

"Oh . . . ," said Elliot. And then he said, "Then why . . . did we run . . . so fast?"

"Because you . . . were running," Fauna replied. "And I . . . didn't want . . . to get left . . . behind."

CHAPTER TWENTY-NINE

The three walked back toward school.

"You think we should check on Bonechewer?" Uchenna asked. "He got bounced around a lot in my bag."

"Let's not check until we're somewhere safe," Elliot said. "Also, his name is Jersey."

Fauna smiled. "Jersey is a very cute name for a Jersey Devil. Not very imaginative. But very cute."

"I like Bonechewer," said Uchenna.

"Really?" said Fauna.

"Or Eyeball-Eater?"

Fauna made a face.

"I was also thinking Gutmuncher the Orphan-Maker."

Fauna pursed his lips. After a moment, he said, "I prefer Jersey."

Elliot raised his skinny arms in the air. "Victory!"

Uchenna frowned.

Then Elliot said, "But we still don't know what we're going to do with him."

Professor Fauna cleared his throat. It sounded like boulders falling down a mountain. "Children, I request that you delay that decision for a moment. I would like to . . . to show you something. It is in my office."

Elliot began to stammer. "Uh, I don't think . . . You see, my mom . . . And the time . . ."

But Uchenna was already shrugging and saying, "Okay."

Elliot gave her a *c'mon-really?* look, but she didn't seem to notice.

So he just muttered, "Sure. Great."

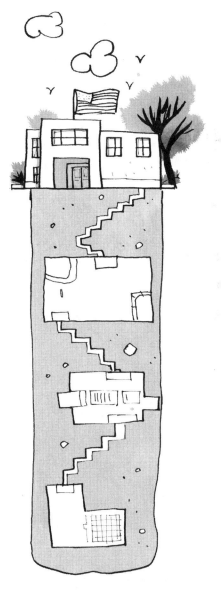

A few minutes later, they passed through the large front doors of the school, going by the security desk, down some stairs, down some more stairs, and down still more stairs, until they were three levels underground. The hallways down here were not lined with linoleum like in the rest of the school, but were dirty, rough concrete. Heat pipes and boilers loomed from the shadows, and an air compressor groaned angrily.

"This is not good," Elliot muttered.

Uchenna didn't reply.

He nudged her. "Uchenna, we shouldn't—"

But she whispered, *"Elliot, I want to see."*

"Great!" Elliot grumbled. "The death wish returns!" Though, if he admitted it to himself, he wanted to see if it was a torture chamber, too. Unless it *was*. Then he didn't want to.

Professor Fauna led them to a small green door. Five locks ran down one side. Professor Fauna

removed a ring of keys from his tweed jacket and unlocked the bolts, one by one. Then he turned the old doorknob and pushed the door open.

"Children," he said, "welcome to my office."

CHAPTER THIRTY

It was not a torture chamber.

But it was very, very strange.

The entire floor of the office was no bigger than a kid's mattress. Not that they could *see* the floor. It was covered with papers, with open books, with scattered maps, with pieces of twine and tape and loose thumbtacks. There was one small desk and one small chair, but no one could sit on the chair or write at the desk, because they were just as cluttered as the floor. Bookshelves

ran from the floor to the ceiling, crammed with the oldest, strangest, most random collection of books either child had ever seen.

"Whoa," Elliot murmured.

"Cool," Uchenna breathed.

Elliot walked directly to the nearest bookshelf. He examined the titles of the books. Among them were:

The Book of Beasts: A Medieval Bestiary, translated from the Latin by T. H. White.

The Natural History of Unicorns, by Chris Lavers.

Pansey Parker's Totally Extreme Unicorn Adventure! by nobody, apparently, but published by Brain Rot Press.

Uchenna was looking at a piece of parchment pinned to the wall above the desk. It was insanely old and looked like a list of names. In a corner of the parchment was a thick wax seal, with an image of a unicorn in the middle of it and Latin words above and below. At the top of the page ran the words: *SOLLEMNIS ORDO UNICORNIS*.

She turned to the professor, who was eyeing the children. He looked pensive. "What is this place?" Uchenna asked. "What do you do here?"

The professor sighed. He put his finger and his thumb on the bridge of his large nose. "I cannot believe I am going to do this."

Elliot took a step back. "Do what?" He glanced around for instruments of torture.

"I said I would not," Professor Fauna went on, ignoring him. He stepped in front of the door, barring their way out. "I said I never would again. Not after the last time."

"Professor, what are you talking about?" Uchenna demanded. She could not stop her voice from rising. "What are you going to do?"

He began to lock the dead bolts, one by one.

"I am going to . . . to tell you a secret. It is a secret known by no one else in this town. Well, almost no one."

"Secrets can be dangerous," Elliot said. "I think a teacher told me that once."

Professor Fauna smiled sadly. He looked as if he were about to give away something he cherished.

"I am the leader of a secret society. We have members all over the world. Our mission is to protect mythical creatures from danger."

"Wait, what?" said Uchenna. Elliot suddenly remembered all the rumors about the professor. *Oh*, he thought. *Right. He's totally unhinged from reality.*

Professor Fauna reached out, his hand facing down. On his ring finger was a large, silver ring. In its center was the carved image of a unicorn. Above the image ran the words *Defende Fabulosa*. Under it ran *Protege Mythica*.

"Okay," Elliot said skeptically. "What is that supposed to mean?"

"*Defende Fabulosa*," said the professor, "means 'Defend the Imaginary.' *Protege Mythica* means 'Protect the Mythical.' My group's mission is to protect creatures that science refuses to recognize. We are called . . . the *Unicorn Rescue Society*."

Uchenna said, "Uhhhh, you rescue *unicorns*?"

"I have never yet found a unicorn, actually," Fauna replied.

"Wait," said Elliot. "It's called the *Unicorn Rescue Society*, but you don't actually rescue unicorns?"

The professor thrust a finger in the air. "It is my *intention* to rescue them!"

"But you've never seen one," said Uchenna.

"Well, no—"

Elliot furrowed his brow. "And yet you still call it the *Unicorn—*"

"Why must you rub it in? One day I will see a unicorn, and the society's destiny will be fulfilled!"

"Only if you rescue it," Uchenna pointed out.

"Right. Of course. Anyway, I have rescued hundreds of creatures, in every corner of the globe. And I have friends who help me, everywhere I go."

"Like Dr. Thomas?" Elliot said, remembering her ring.

"Indeed, like Dr. Thomas. She is helping me protect the creatures of the Pine Barrens. One creature in particular."

Uchenna unzipped her backpack. She tilted it forward.

The little Jersey Devil poked his head out into the light.

The professor laughed. "A young Jersey Devil—look at him! Marvelous!" Jersey tilted his head up to get a better angle on the professor. Then he said, "I *still* cannot believe I am about to do this."

"Do what?" Elliot and Uchenna said at once.

Professor Fauna took a deep breath. "My secret society is in danger. We have enemies. The Schmoke brothers in particular. They are defeating us. Threatening the creatures of myth and legend. And the world is changing. Our secret society is on the verge of extinction, just as the animals we protect. We need help. We need youth. We need . . . you."

Elliot looked surprised. Uchenna looked surprised. Even Jersey looked surprised.

"You may not have listened to me in the Pine Barrens. But you listened to the cry of this little creature. You were kind enough. And brave enough. I threatened you—but you helped him anyway. You faced the Schmoke brothers and did not waver. This is what we need. Courage. Strength. Kindness. Courage."

"You said 'courage' twice," Elliot pointed out.

"We need lots of courage," Fauna replied. "So, will you join me? Elliot? Uchenna? And that Jersey

Devil there, who is now, most surely, yours?"

Jersey sat up a little straighter in the backpack.

"Will you join us?" Professor Fauna held out his ring once more. "Will you join the Unicorn Rescue Society?"

Elliot did not move.

Uchenna did not move.

Each child was thinking, *Is this for real? Can I trust this guy? What would my parents say? I'm scared. I'm excited. I think I can feel my heart beating in my neck. Maybe I'm having a heart attack. And hallucinating. Maybe this whole day has been a hallucination.*

Still, neither spoke.

And then Jersey leaned toward Professor Fauna's outstretched hand—and licked it.

Elliot, Uchenna, and Professor Fauna all stared. Then they started laughing. Jersey looked back and forth, from one human to the other, confused.

"I guess that's a *yes*?" Uchenna said with a laugh.

"I think that's a *yes*," Elliot agreed.

Professor Fauna exhaled. Then he grinned.

"Welcome, *mis amigos*, to the Unicorn Rescue Society."

To Be Continued

ACKNOWLEDGMENTS

Just as it requires a network of people around the world to protect the creatures of myth and legend, so does it require a network of people around the world to create the Unicorn Rescue Society series, and this book in particular. We'd like to thank *everyone* who helped us share the amazing exploits of the Unicorn Rescue Society, but particularly we'd like to thank:

Ryan Downer, who read the manuscript with care and whose grandmother was an inspiration.

John Volpa, for your expertise in the ecology and history of the Pine Barrens.

Dr. Frank Esposito, distinguished professor of history and education at Kean University, and author of the forthcoming *Secret History of the Jersey Devil*, for your comprehensive knowledge of New Jersey's history—and that of our little blue friend.

Dr. J. R. Norwood, of the Nanticoke Lenni-Lenape Tribal Nation, for your kindness, encouragement, and guidance.

Uncle Rick, also known as Dr. Richard A. LaFleur, Franklin Professor of Classics at the University of Georgia and editor of *Wheelock's Latin* (as well as the best eccentric uncle you could ask for).

Olugbemisola Rhuday-Perkovich, for the time you spent on early pages and character formation.

Tracey Baptiste, who read the initial drafts, revised passages with subtlety and insight, and, in the process, suggested the term "medley."

Joseph Bruchac, Emma Otheguy, and David Bowles, for your corrections, insight, and for joining the quest! *Defende Fabulosa!*

Sarah Burnes, who is our big sister and den mother. We'd be lost without you.

Eddie Gamarra, for your infinite patience and unflinching advice.

Julie Strauss-Gabel, truly the most insightful editor on the planet, and the amazing team at Penguin Young Readers. A special shout-out to the marketing team, who inspired our first line.

An extra-special shout-out to Anna Booth, who made this book as beautiful as it is.

Rosanne Lauer, copyeditor extraordinaire (and a darn good English stylist, too).

Hatem Aly, of course, whose art is an inspiration.

To the real Uchenna and "Elliot." You know who you are. We hope these characters do even a modicum of justice to your actual awesomeness.

And finally, a very special thank you to the third and fourth graders at Frog Pond Elementary and George J. Mitchell Elementary in the Pine Barrens, and to their generous and enthusiastic teachers, who read this book and gave us their feedback. We hope it makes you proud.

Adam Gidwitz taught big kids and not-so-big kids in Brooklyn for eight years. Now he spends most of his time chronicling the adventures of the Unicorn Rescue Society. He is also the author of the Newbery Honor–winning *The Inquisitor's Tale,* as well as the best-selling *A Tale Dark and Grimm* and its companions.

Jesse Casey and **Chris Smith** are filmmakers. They founded Mixtape Club, an award-winning production company in New York City, where they make videos and animations for all sorts of people.

Adam and Jesse met when they were eleven years old. They have done many things together, like building a car powered only by a mousetrap and inventing two board games. Jesse and Chris met when they were eighteen years old. They have done many things together, too, like making music videos for rock bands and an animation for the largest digital billboard ever. But Adam and Jesse and Chris wanted to do something *together*. First, they made trailers for Adam's books. Then they made a short film together. And now they are sharing with the world the courage, curiosity, kindness, and courage of the members of the Unicorn Rescue Society!

Hatem Aly is an Egyptian-born illustrator whose work has been featured in multiple publications worldwide. He currently lives in New Brunswick, Canada, with his wife, son, and more pets than people. Find him online at metahatem.com or @metahatem.

PHOTO CREDIT: Michelle Pinet

Turn the page for a sneak preview
of the Unicorn Rescue Society's
next adventure!

CHAPTER ONE

Elliot Eisner was lying, facedown, on the pavement in front of his new house, in his new town, in New Jersey.

The morning was clear and fine. Kids were walking past on their way to school, kicking red and yellow leaves. It smelled of fall.

Why was Elliot lying facedown on the pavement?

He wasn't sure. He had opened his front door, stepped on something, and then gone toppling headfirst down the steps. Elliot pushed himself up and turned around to see what he had tripped on.

On his front step was a small package, wrapped in brown paper. He got to his feet and walked over to the package. No address. No stamps. Just a name, scrawled in brown ink. Weird. He examined the name on the package.

It was his name.

Elliot had had a *strange* day yesterday. It had been his first day at his new school. He'd made a friend, Uchenna Devereaux. She was strange. She kinda dressed like a punk rocker, she made up random songs about nothing at all, and she had a strong desire to put herself, and Elliot, in mortal danger. All that said, she was funny and she was brave and Elliot liked her. They had rescued a young Jersey Devil—which was supposed to be an imaginary creature, but definitely was *not* imaginary.

It seemed to have adopted them. Finally, a terrifying teacher at their school, named Professor Fauna, had invited them to join a secret organization: the Unicorn Rescue Society. Its mission was to save mythical creatures from danger.

So yeah, it had been a strange day.

Now Elliot was staring at a mysterious package that had been left on his doorstep.

For him.

He tore open the paper. A book stared up at him. *The Country of Basque.*

"What?" Elliot said out loud, to no one.

Why had someone left him a book? On his doorstep? And who had left it? And couldn't he just have a normal, not-at-all dangerous second day at South Pines Elementary? Please?

He sighed, tucked the book under his arm, threw his backpack over his shoulder, and started off to school.

CHAPTER TWO

Uchenna Devereaux normally left her house with one shoe untied, half her homework still under the bed upstairs, playing air guitar, and singing a song she'd made up that morning in the shower.

But not today.

She opened her front door and looked down her street in both directions before slipping out into the cool autumn morning. She put her backpack over her shoulders, pulled the straps tight, and began walking, warily, to school. Yesterday had been a weird day.

She had made a new friend named Elliot. He wasn't exactly *cool*—he got nervous easily, he memorized entire books about things that could kill him, and he was definitely *not* rock-and-roll. But he was smart and funny, and Uchenna liked him. Also, they'd met a Jersey Devil and been invited by the school's weirdest teacher to join a secret society. This secret society had very rich and very powerful enemies: the Schmoke brothers, two billionaires who owned businesses all over the world, and half their little town.

Also, Uchenna and Elliot and that weird teacher *may* have broken into the Schmoke brothers' mansion.

Okay, they definitely did.

Which was why Uchenna was being so vigilant this morning on her walk to school. As she turned the corner from her block onto the main street, she glanced over her shoulder. A few blocks away lay the wealthiest neighborhood in town—where the Schmoke brothers' mansion was. Beyond that, in the distance, she could barely make out the towering smokestacks of the Schmoke Industries power plant, billowing black plumes into the air. She—*FTHUMP!*

Uchenna sat down hard on her rear end. A small, thin boy with curly brown hair was lying on his back on the sidewalk, staring up into space. An open book lay on the sidewalk behind him.

"Elliot!" Uchenna exclaimed.

"Ow," said Elliot.

"I didn't see you there!"

"That's good. The alternative would have been that you *did* see me there and ambushed me on purpose."

Uchenna laughed and got to her feet. "Come on. Let's get to school."

Elliot lay unmoving on the ground. "I don't think so. Today's been pretty messed up already. School's only going to make it worse."

Uchenna grabbed Elliot by the wrist and pulled him to his feet. She scooped up *The Country of Basque* and handed it to him. "Let's go. However messed up today's going to be, it'll be better if we face it together."

As Elliot brushed off his khaki pants, he squinted at Uchenna. "Your positivity disgusts me."

Uchenna grinned, threw her arm around Elliot's neck, and dragged him toward school.

CHAPTER THREE

Elliot and Uchenna sat at the far end of one of the long tables in the school cafeteria, waiting for the morning bell to ring. Kids were streaming in the double doors, finding their friends, laughing, clowning, discussing whatever they'd seen on television or online the night before.

Not Elliot and Uchenna, though. Elliot was telling Uchenna about the mysterious book on his doorstep. "I haven't read much of it yet. Just the first five chapters."

"You read the first five chapters between your house and the corner where we knocked into each other? That's one block!"

"They're short chapters. And I read pretty fast."

"So, what did you learn?"

"Well, I learned about the Basque people, the Euskaldunak."

"The yoos-KAHL-juh-nak?"

"Yeah. They're kinda amazing. They're these fierce mountain people, who've lived nestled between Spain and France and the sea, for thousands of years. Pretty much every great empire of Europe has tried to conquer them, but no one could."

"They sound awesome."

"Definitely."

"Any idea *why* you're reading this book? Or who gave it to you?"

"I have two guesses. Both frighten me."

Uchenna shrugged. "You *are* easily frightened."

"One possibility is the Schmoke brothers."

"Okay," Uchenna said, "that would frighten

me, too. But why would the Schmoke brothers leave you a *book*?"

"No idea. A warning? The other person who could have left it for me is—"

At that very moment, the cafeteria doors crashed open, and in strode a tall, wiry man with a black-and-white beard and a shock of hair exploding from his skull. He wore an old tweed suit and shoes that had probably been expensive forty years ago. From under his shaggy eyebrows, his eyes roved the faces of the nearby students—who cowered before him.

Which was not surprising, because he looked like he might attack someone.

The man's name was Professor Mito Fauna.

"The other possibility," Elliot continued, subtly gesturing at the man, who was now peering around the cafeteria as if he were looking for his next victim, "is him."